ABOUT THE BOOK / ABOUT THE AUTHOR

What if you heard about a children's book, partly inspired by Sept. 11, that is changing American children's lives?

That's inspiring them to write poetry, create poignant artwork, and give of themselves to other children? That's providing healing to children who saw the hijacked planes hit the World Trade Center towers and the buildings collapse?

What if you heard that proceeds from this children's book have supported homeless children in Nicaragua, and orphaned children in Uganda? And that sales of this book are helping to keep alive a mother of five who has AIDS?

What if you heard that grandparents are snapping up this children's book for themselves, and not their grandchildren? That its message is so powerful it's being consumed by parents who have problems with their teen-agers, and by adults going through divorce, and those who counsel troubled children?

Would you want to read such a book?

What if you heard that this book, after being introduced to jittery new immigrants in an ESL class, "melted away fears, brought healing, understanding, and pride in being part of a new wave of American society?"

What if you heard that the story about the book is as interesting as the book? For instance, the author first sold 13 copies at a fundraiser. But sales really took off in Indiana, at her mother's beauty salon. Meanwhile, back in New Jersey, an AKA sorority member who had bought one copy returned for 55 more for children in a group home. A few weeks later, a philanthropist and his wife purchased one copy for their grandson, and after reading it, instantly decided to buy nearly 2,000 more for local elementary school children.

"Kara Finds Sunshine on a Rainy Day" is that book.

"Kara Finds Sunshine on a Rainy Day" is a book of hope and healing for children, AND adults. It grew out of "The Sun is Always Shining," a poem the author wrote about 10 days after the Sept. 11, 2001 terrorist attacks. She was trying to find an uplifting theme to present to young mothers who would be participating in a workshop with her for 7 weeks.

In the book, a child is introduced to heroes of all races and backgrounds, and she ultimately learns that with faith, hope, and love, we can become our own heroes in difficult situations. With "Kara", first-time author Caroline Brewer soundly and gracefully goes about her mission to make the world a better place. Readers will close the book on "Kara" and be filled with a sense of hope about the world and their place in it.

In July 2001, Caroline Brewer left an award winning 16-year-career in journalism, which included stints in TV, radio, public relations, newspapers, and service on two Pulitzer Prize juries, to start an inspirational services company. Her company, Unchained Spirit Enterprises, hosts motivational seminars for professionals, the unemployed, underemployed, groups and organizations, teens and children. She has also performed poetry and spoken word presentations before audiences in churches and cultural centers.

Kara Finds Sunshine on a Rainy Day

Written by:
Caroline Brewer

Designed by:
Samantha Spitaletta

Illustrations by:

Thamina Ahmed – Kim Phuc, Brooklyn, NY
Cerita Asante – Pentagon, Teaneck, NJ
Eman Bani – Harriet Tubman Portrait
Zajiir Barrett – Border Sun, Paterson, NJ
Nyesha Brimley – Large Pink Heart, Paterson, NJ
Jamar Byrd – A. Philip Randolph, Brooklyn, NY
Jasmine Cappe – Sitting Bull, Brooklyn, NY
Khiya Carlington – Playground and Rain, Westwood, NJ
Flavia Cojocaria – Helen Keller, Herndon, VA
Aaron Dunbar – Mahatma Gandhi, Herndon, VA
LaVraea Eldridge – House and Rain, Fort Wayne, IN
Warren Fields – WTC Towers, Teaneck, NJ
Gabrielle Frankel – Anne Frank, Westwood, NJ

Jasmine Glaze – Kara and Red, Yellow, Orange Sun, Kara/Mom Standing, Kara/Mom sitting, Sun with sunglasses, Elkart, IN
Nyshon Green – Lady on the Bus, Newark & Paterson, NJ
Melina Hassiotti – Pointy-Ray Sun, Westwood, NJ
Rosemari Interiano – Rosy-Cheeked Sun, Westwood, NJ
Raven Jones – French Villagers, Teaneck, NJ
Samantha Justiano – Oklahoma City Children, Teaneck, NJ
Sydni Lester – Murrah Federal Building and Teddy Bears, Teaneck, NJ
Juan Martinez – Cesar Chavez, Westwood, NJ
Billy Metz – Orange Sun, Westwood, NJ
Lamir Murray – Slender Fuscia Hearts, Paterson, NJ

Eli Ostroff – Harriet Tubman & Freedom-seekers, Teaneck, NJ
Anirudh Rallabhandi – Teardrop-Ray Sun, Westwood, NJ
Angelica Rodriguez – Children Holding Hands, Paterson, NJ
Tony Simmons – Page Number Sun, Paterson, NJ
Kevin Song – Dull Knife & Buffaloes, Westwood, NJ
Latrice Tate – Helen Keller, Paterson, NJ
Breyonia Trent – Many red hearts, Paterson, NJ
Shayla Trent – Page Number Heart, Paterson, NJ
Kevin Venkatesh – World Trade Towers in flames, Westwood, NJ
Emily Ann Wacha – Rosa Parks Teaneck, NJ
Georgianna Williams – Border Blue-eyed Sun, Paterson, NJ

Unchained Spirit Enterprises, Teaneck, NJ

Published by:
Unchained Spirit Enterprises
P.O. Box 52
Teaneck, NJ 07666

ISBN: 0-9717790-2-3

Printed in the USA
Book Design: Samantha Spitaletta
Cover: Jasmine Glaze and Caroline Brewer

DEDICATIONS & ACKNOWLEDGMENTS

This book is dedicated to the students and staff of Paterson's Adult School, all the family members of victims of the terrorist attacks, to my 4-year-old great-niece Tykara Howard, my second-cousins Christay, Christan, and Vasco Smith, my god-daughter Jasmine Glaze, and to all of the world's children.

I'd also like to dedicate this book to all of the people who have helped keep the sun shining in my life. They are too numerous to name, but I must, first of all, my mother, Ethel Brewer. She has been the sun in my life for the whole of my life, and the mother in this book represents her loving, optimistic spirit in truth. I thank also my daughters, Christian and Danielle Brewer, for lots of help during a challenging summer of promotion, my brother, Glenn Brewer, sisters Liz Howard and Diane Brewer; great friends, Georgia and Philip Glaze, Ketu Oladuwa, Vince Robinson, Lisa Goodnight, Georgette Delinois, Stacy Foster, Rose Simmons, Jackie Sergeant, Frankye Regis, Veona Thomas, Johanne Reid, Lawrence Aaron, Yvette Moy, Liz Llorente, Maia Davis, Vivian Waixel; Ann Bennett and AKA - Bergen County, and Vera Stokes and Chi Eta Phi, Tau Chi Chapter of nurses.

Secondly, I thank my pastor, Rev. Randall M. Lassiter and all the members of Greater Faith Church of the Abundance, for so lovingly and enthusiastically supporting this book and me every step of the way.

I am grateful also for three exceptional friends; Angeline Hall-Watts, a second-grade teacher who encouraged me to write a version of "The Sun is Always Shining" for young children. Because of her urging, this book was born, and Angeline and her wonderful network of sister-friends have helped spread its message throughout northern New Jersey.

I am delighted also to express my sincere appreciation to Dr. Alfred Fayemi, an author of beautiful photography books, who has been my mentor, my advisor, my shoulder to cry on, and more during this book's life. Dr. Fayemi also gave the book a reason for being. After returning from Uganda in October, 2001, he told me about the wonderful people working on shoestring budgets to support children orphaned because of AIDS. He set up a charity for them and in December, 2001, I held a fundraiser for the charity. A month later, I began sending $100 a month (based on sales of this book) for medication to a Ugandan mother of five who has AIDS.

I'm tickled to also thank my "big brother and sister," Lonnie and Debra Youngblood. Through the worst of times, they kept me laughing, and through the best of times, they kept me smiling. Their love, their friendship, their enthusiastic promotion of the book helped eased the inevitable challenges that arose along the way. They are wonderful friends to have on any day, but especially on a rainy day.

I thank with all my heart Perry and Gladys Rosenstein, and Tim Blunk, of the Puffin Foundation, Ltd., for instant and generous support, which got the book into the hands of nearly 4,000 children and their teachers. Their support – which twice was offered out of the blue – came at critical times, and frankly, helped keep the lights on and the rent paid.

I am honored to also thank the more than 100 children who submitted illustrations for this edition of the book, as well as their instructional leaders: Lucille Amorosi Maas, Hawthorne Elementary in Teaneck; Angeline Hall-Watts, Berkeley Elementary in Westwood; Tiffany Bryant at Herndon Elementary in Herndon, Va.; Sandra McRae at P.S. 32, Brooklyn; Irma Gorham at the Paterson Housing Authority; and Della McCall-Williams and Cassandra Mitchell at Trust in Us Afterschool in Paterson.

I am most grateful as well for the thousands of people who bought earlier editions of the book – on street corners, at book parties, bookstores, libraries, schools, churches, community centers, and from my mother and daughters. You encouraged me in ways for which I cannot find adequate words.

I thank Mr. Robert Small, of Harlem, for welcoming my daughters and me onto his property and into his community of street vendors during a hot summer when my money was at its lowest. God bless your generous soul.

I thank also Samantha Spitaletta, the graphic artist for this book, for patiently working with me through all of the editions over 9 months, and making my ideas become real.

In closing, I thank God for inspiring this book in me. It has revolutionized my life, my thinking, and given me a whole new reason for being. My most sincere hope is that all who read this book will become childlike in their willingness to focus on all the good there is in life, especially in times of trouble.

Caroline Brewer
President, Unchained Spirit Enterprises™

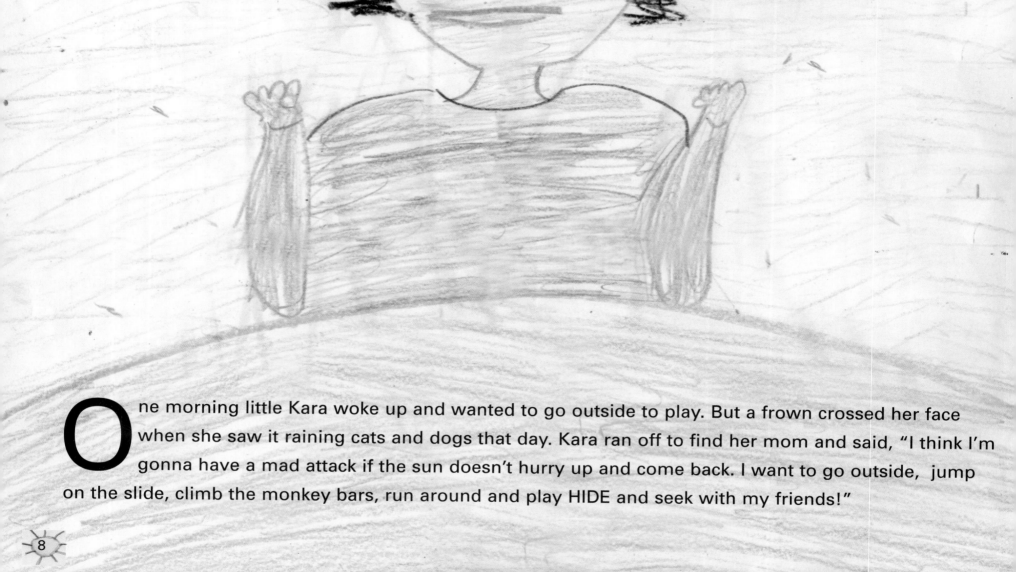

One morning little Kara woke up and wanted to go outside to play. But a frown crossed her face when she saw it raining cats and dogs that day. Kara ran off to find her mom and said, "I think I'm gonna have a mad attack if the sun doesn't hurry up and come back. I want to go outside, jump on the slide, climb the monkey bars, run around and play HIDE and seek with my friends!"

Her mom told her, "Darling,
there is something important
that you should know:
whether there's rain outside,
or sleet, or snow,
the sun is always shining."

The sun shines day and night.
It spreads its rays
from the highest heights.
It beams through clouds and rain.
It comes to our rescue
when we're in pain.
The sun is always shining.

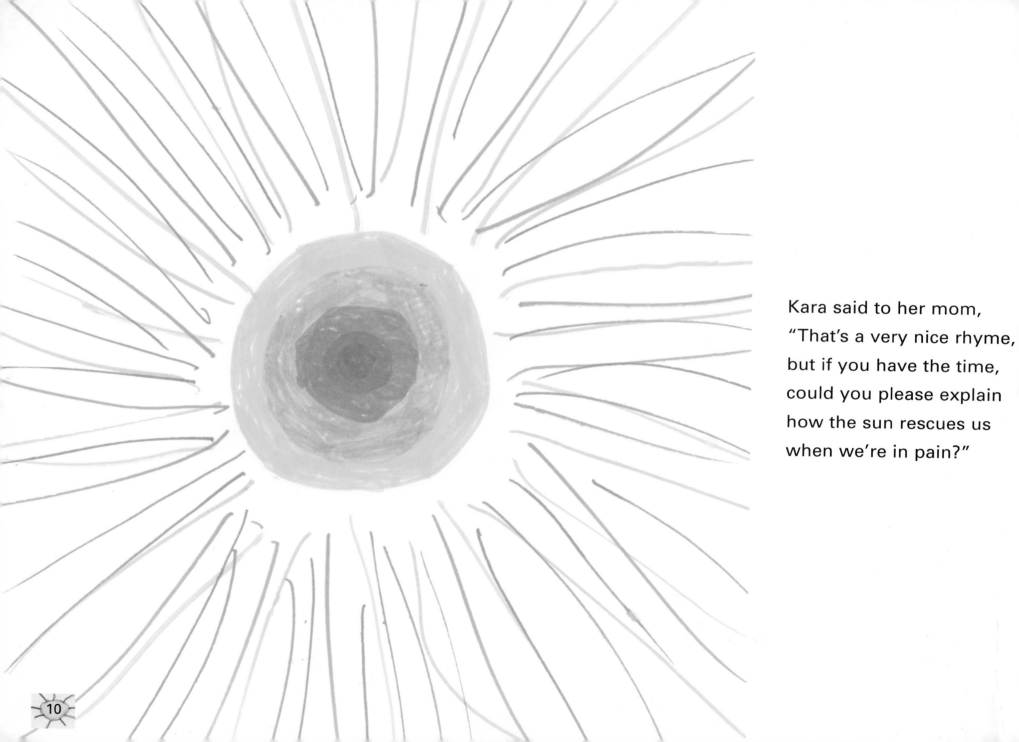

Kara said to her mom,
"That's a very nice rhyme,
but if you have the time,
could you please explain
how the sun rescues us
when we're in pain?"

Her mom said: "Darling, life is made up of joy and pain. It's got sunshine and it's got rain. We need the sun and rain to grow fruit and vegetables, and the leafy green trees that give us shade. That's just the wondrous way our earth was made.

When things go wrong, our insides feel like thunder and rain. Then someone comes along and does something nice for us. They represent the sun, and sweetly lift away our pain.

Or we start to look at our pain a little differently, and become our own sun. If we find the strength to do something nice for others, pretty soon the darkness in our hearts will be gone."

"Gee, mom, I never thought of sunshine and rain that way," Kara said. "Do you have any more stories, since it's still too wet for me to go outside, jump on the slide, climb the monkey bars, run around and play HIDE and seek with my friends?"

"I certainly do my sweet child," replied Kara's mom. "To share more stories with my curious little girl will only make my heart proud."

Back in the 1950s, Rosa Parks was a lady who was sad, because black people in the South were being treated badly by segregation – laws that kept blacks and whites from sitting or eating together, no matter the place, time, or weather. One day Rosa Parks refused to sit in the back of the bus, where blacks were told to go. That made the Alabamans huff and puff. But this one lady's courage helped get the laws changed so that from then on blacks and whites had to be treated the same.

Cesar Chavez worked on a farm, where people of Mexican heritage were often harmed by long days of hard work for just a little pay.

Mr. Chavez decided to stand up for his rights and say that all farm workers need better jobs and health care so they can take care of their families.

He is remembered today for helping to improve life for so many poor people in a very special and non-violent way.

Mahatma Gandhi was a kind and gentle prince, who wore no crown.

His kingdom was not about money, or putting others down. His actions and beliefs were all about peace.

His love for every one helped free millions of Indian people in a revolution that was won without the firing of a single gun.

It's just one more
example of how
the sun shines day
and night.
Spreads its rays
from the
highest heights.

Of how it beams
through clouds
and rain.

Comes to our rescue
when we're in pain.

The sun is always shining.

During World War II, André Trocmé gathered a group of French villagers, who risked their lives to save Jews.

You may recall Anne Frank,
a teenager who kept a diary
that helps us learn the truth
about how badly people were
treated during the war.

Even though she died,
she expressed a lot of love
and hope for humankind.

Harriet Tubman had a secret chariot.

It swung down low and helped slaves get to freedom on the Underground Railroad.

21

Native Americans had many proud chiefs, such as Little Wolf, Sitting Bull, and Dull Knife.

Little Wolf showed courage and honor in his fight to save the Cheyenne people's lives.

Sitting Bull was a loving, friendly man who went to his grave being known also as very brave.

Dull Knife had a lot of skills.
As a child he saved his younger sister
from being **killed** by a buffalo stampede.

Helen Keller was deaf and blind
but she had faith in things not seen.

She learned to talk, and helped
all people see that no matter
their challenges they could cope,
and be, like sunshine, a ray of hope.

Kim Phuc was a 9-year-old Vietnamese girl when she was burned by a bomb explosion in a war. It made her whole body sore.

Now she is a wife and mother of two boys, and her life is full of joy. Because she practices forgiveness and peace even for the man who hurt her, in hopes that one day all wars will cease.

The sun shines day and night.
Spreads it rays
from the highest heights.
It beams through clouds and rain.
Comes to our rescue
when we're in pain.
The sun is always shining.

A. Philip Randolph was a writer and freedom fighter. His desire for fairness knew no borders. It led him to start a union for Sleeping Car Porters.

He got President Roosevelt and President Truman to change laws that had discrimination flaws.

He founded the March on Washington, where Martin Luther King told the world he had a dream. A. Philip Randolph was always on the scene to help out his fellow human being.

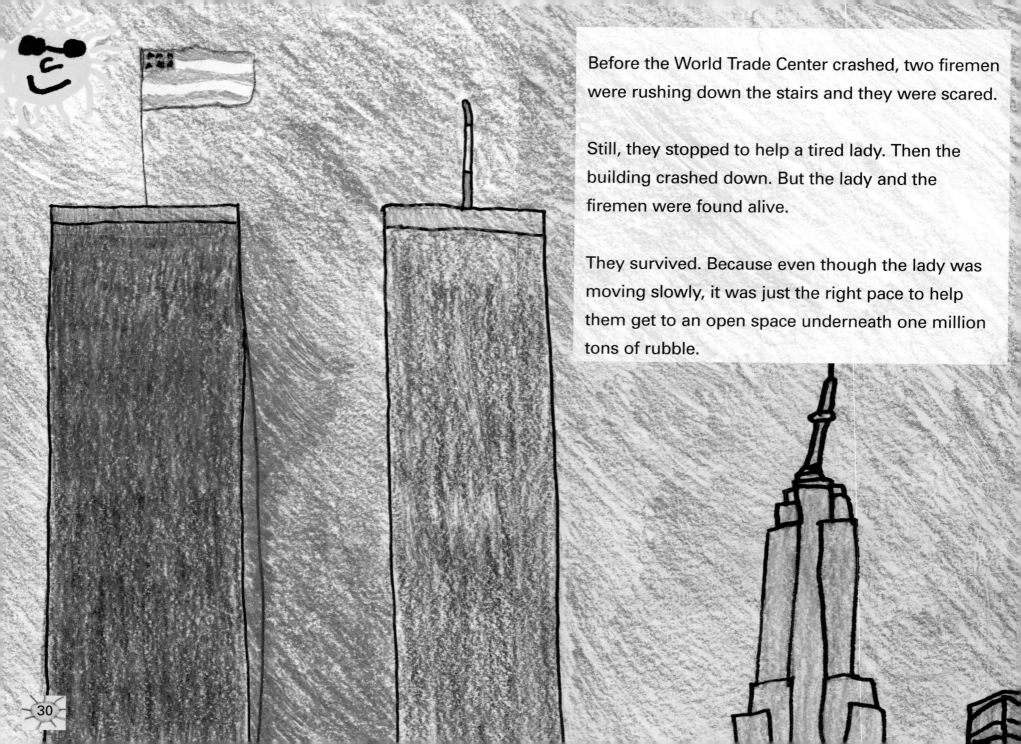

Before the World Trade Center crashed, two firemen were rushing down the stairs and they were scared.

Still, they stopped to help a tired lady. Then the building crashed down. But the lady and the firemen were found alive.

They survived. Because even though the lady was moving slowly, it was just the right pace to help them get to an open space underneath one million tons of rubble.

After the attack in New York City, and on the Pentagon in Washington, D.C., a child sold her toys and gave the money to little girls and boys, who had lost a parent.

Children from Oklahoma City sent teddy bears and cards.

They had been through something like this before, and knew it would be hard.

"Wow, mom," little Kara said.
"I didn't realize there were so many
stories of how sunshine can help
rescue us from pain."

"Yes, darling," replied mom,
"There are lots of stories about people
who became great in difficult times.
If we just keep our hearts open,
they'll be easy to find."

"You see, the symbol of peace is a
dove. The heart is a picture of love.

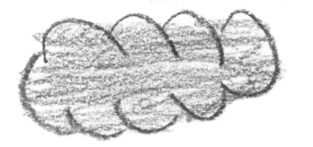

So sometimes when we're sad, it helps if we reach out and touch somebody's hand, and continue to make the world a better place for every child, woman and man."

Because the sun shines day and night. Spreads it rays from the highest heights.

It beams through clouds and rain.
It comes to our rescue when we're in pain.
The sun is always shining.

Kara Finds Sunshine on a Rainy Day

GUIDE FOR TEACHERS, PARENTS AND YOUTH LEADERS

One of the ways to reinforce the message of this book is to talk to your children about Joy, Pain, Hope and Healing. It's especially appropriate after something sad or tragic happens, whether it happens in school, in the community, or somewhere else in the world. It also might be helpful to put the discussion in the context of Heroes.

Here's an example based on discussions I have with children's groups.

1) Explain what Pain, Joy, Hope and Healing are, and ask your students to give you examples of such things in their life. Here are some of my examples.

Joy is something that makes you smile. For instance, Kara feels joy when she goes outside to play with friends. Spending time with a grandparent or favorite aunt or uncle can be a joyous thing. Eating a meal at your favorite restaurant. Having a sleepover and watching your favorite movies with friends. Reading your favorite book. Singing. Dancing. Riding a bike. All of these things can bring you joy.

Pain is something that makes you feel sad or bad. Getting a bad grade is painful. When someone calls you a bad name, that's painful. It's painful if a friend hits you, or a brother or sister takes your favorite toy. It's painful if someone you love dies.

Hope is something that you want to happen that makes you smile. If a birthday is coming up, you feel hopeful. Or a special holiday or a visit to a close friend or family member. If you're going to take a field trip in school to a fun place, like a museum or an amusement park, you feel hopeful about it.

Healing is when you feel better after experiencing pain. When the adult who loves you kisses your knee after you fall from a bike, that's a form of healing. When a family member or friend brings you soup when you

have a cold, that's helps you heal and feel better. When someone gives you a hug when you're having a bad day, that's healing. When you make up with a friend, or brother or sister after a fight, that's healing.

2) Explain to your children that if we could put Joy, Pain, Hope, and Healing into separate jars, and we adults had to choose which things we'd want in our life each day, we would always choose from the jar of Joy. However, real life is not like that, as demonstrated by the real-life people in "Kara Finds Sunshine On A Rainy Day." Painful things happen. Not every day; but every now and then. So it's important that we find ways to cope with pain and heal from it, the same way we cope with and heal from pain from a cut or a scrape. Painful situations also are what make heroes -- in real life, as well as the movies and comics. It's from pain that we find the hero in each of us.

3) Depending on how much time you have, ask your children to contribute to a list of 5 or 10 things that they find joyful, and 5 or 10 things they find painful or sad.

Go through each item with your children. When you talk about the joyful item, ask them to explain how they can share their joy with someone else. When you talk about each painful item, ask them to think of ways that they might heal from the pain, and become their own sun (or hero). For instance, one child told me that failing in school would be a painful thing. But she could become her own sun, her own hero in other words, by studying much harder and getting better grades.

I offered the example that my niece was once failing her chemistry course. She was in a lot of pain because of it. But she found a classmate to help her study. When the semester was over, she had gone from a failing grade to a B+. Two heroes came out of

this painful situation – my niece found there was a hero in her by not giving up on herself, and she found a hero in her classmate, who gave up her own free time to help my niece study.

In another example, 12 students and one teacher were killed at Columbine High School. About a dozen other students were shot and injured; three of them are now paralyzed. Richard Castaldo was one of those paralyzed.

According to the Rocky-Mountain News of Denver, When Richard was facing his "darkest hours," Nobel Peace Prize laureate Jose Ramos-Horta of East Timor visited his hospital room with a message of hope. Shortly after he got out of the hospital, Richard decided that he wanted to return the favor by leading an effort to help the youngsters of violence-racked East Timor restore their schools.

"About a week after I was shot ... Jose Ramos-Horta visited me when I was in the hospital, and I was very grateful for this support and friendship," Richard reportedly said. "I have learned that to have friends, you must also be a friend. Wherever you live, everything is interconnected. What happens in Denver affects Tibet and affects Africa, it affects East Timor."

The shooting at Columbine was the worst school shooting in American history. Yet, out of the pain of that situation, a young man who was paralyzed decided that he could still make a contribution to needy children in another part of the world – a part of the world most of us know nothing about. There's no doubt that Richard Castaldo represents the sun in his own life, and is a hero to many who know him.

When I was a journalist, I came across many stories of real-life, ordinary heroes. One story involved a 7-year-old girl who died of a brain tumor. The little girl's cancer was discovered when she was 5. She loved to draw

rainbows, and even after the cancer showed up, the little girl kept drawing rainbows. To her parents, the rainbows were like a message of hope. They made the little girl smile, and they made her parents smile. After the little girl died, her parents started a charity to help other families cope with having a terminally ill child. Its symbol is a rainbow.

Another story involved a 12-year-old boy who has cerebral palsy. The boy with cerebral palsy can't walk, talk, bathe, or feed himself. But he has a great smile and that inspired a teacher to adopt him. The teacher and her husband wanted children, but couldn't have any. After taking care of the boy for a couple of years, the teacher gave birth to a child. The boy's natural parents were drug addicts, but after hearing of how their son touched other lives, they gave up their drug addiction and start coming back into his life. So in this case, the fact that the boy had a lot of disabilities was a source of pain. But he used the one thing he had – his big, beautiful smile – to create joy in his life and the lives of others. He became his own sun (hero) and he's a hero to his natural and adopted parents.

4) After you finish with this discussion, ask your children to continue to look for examples of heroes in their school, in their homes and communities, in news reports, and academic subjects. In addition, your children can use the theme of this book, "The sun is always shining," to do art projects or dramatic presentations. For instance, each child can play the role of a historical figure and memorize that person's rhyme. Children can also use this book to learn more about history. They can explore the properties of the sun in science, and explore the homelands of characters to learn about geography. The book can be used to initiate writing projects. Many children have been inspired to write poetry. Let you and your children's imaginations be the guide.

Kara Finds Sunshine on a Rainy Day

GLOSSARY

Cesar Chavez – Born March 31, 1927, on a small farm near Yuma, Arizona, that his grandfather homesteaded during the 1880s. At age 10, his life began as a migrant farm worker when his father lost the land during the Depression.

Chavez founded and led the first successful farm workers' union in U.S. history. When he died April 23, 1993, he was president of the United Farm Workers of America, AFL-CIO. There is a Chavez park in Sacramento, Calif. and a Chavez garden in Albuquerque, N. M. among the many sites honoring this American hero.

Anne Frank – Anne Frank was a German-Jewish teen who was forced, along with her family and four others, to hide out for 2 years in an attic during the Holocaust. She became famous because of the deeply moving diary she kept during her family's ordeal. It was first published in 1947, and today has been translated into 67 languages. Here is one excerpt: "It's a wonder I haven't abandoned all my ideals, they seem so absurd and impractical. Yet I cling to them because I still believe, in spite of everything, that people are truly good at heart."

French Villagers – Le Chambon-sur-Lignon was a remote village of about 2,000 people in south central France in the 1940s. Andre Trocme, the Protestant pastor of Le Chambon, and his wife Magda, built a rescue network in Le Chambon and neighboring villages that helped rescue 5,000 Jews, many of them children, fleeing Nazi terror.

Gandhi – Mohandas K. Gandhi was born in 1869 to Hindu parents in the state of Gujarat in Western India. He fought for better rights for Indians in South Africa for a time and then moved back to India to take the lead in the long struggle for independence from Britain. He believed in only non-violent protest. When Britain gave India its freedom in 1947, "It was not a military victory, but a triumph of human will." It also proved there is great power in good.

Helen Keller – Born June 27, 1880 in Alabama, the daughter of a newspaper editor. In 1882, she caught a fever that was so fierce she nearly died. She lived, but the fever left her without sight or hearing, and made it difficult for her to talk. As she grew older, she became frustrated, wild and unruly because she couldn't speak. But she was given a teacher, Anne Sullivan, who worked hard and patiently to teach her sign language. Helen was so curious, and had such great powers of concentration and memory that she was able to earn several college degrees. After her death in 1968, an organization was set up in her name to combat blindness in the developing world. Today that agency, Helen Keller International, is one of the biggest organizations working with blind people overseas.

Native Americans – Sitting Bull was born in 1831 on the Grand River in present-day South Dakota. He was a Hunkpapa Lakota chief and man of legendary courage. He was the last of his tribe to surrender to American military forces. He died in 1890. He is remembered as an inspirational leader, fearless warrior, loving father, gifted singer, friendly, prophetic, and of deep religious faith.

Dull Knife was a Cheyenne chief, known for his resourcefulness. As a child, he saved his younger sister from a buffalo stampede. Later, he killed a bear with only a dull knife, earning him his name. He also saved his tribe from starvation one harsh winter. When the military campaign began in 1875 to round up Native American tribes and put them on reservations, he refused to give up and died fighting with his tribe.

Little Wolf was a calm and brave Cheyenne chief who led his people out of government confinement, where they had been starving, to new territory in the mountains. The Native Americans only wanted to live in peace on their own land. As they traveled, Little Wolf made his tribe vow to not fire at American military forces before being fired upon. He and his tribe were later captured, but his love for his people and life gave him the strength and courage to fight until the very end.

Rosa Parks – After a long day of work as a seamstress for a Montgomery, Alabama, department store, Rosa Parks boarded a city bus to go home. It was December 1, 1955, and Mrs. Parks was tired as she walked past the mostly empty rows of seats marked, "Whites Only." It was against the law for an African American to sit in those seats. Mrs. Parks sat in a middle section of the bus, but it soon became full. As more whites boarded the bus, she was told to give up her seat. She politely refused. With the support and leadership of Rev. Martin Luther King, Jr., her decision led to a boycott of the buses and eventually to the outlawing of segregation in the South. For a whole year, Montgomery blacks walked to work and shopping, took taxis, or rode with friends in cars to demonstrate their demand to be treated equally. On Dec. 21, 1956, Montgomery's public transportation system was legally integrated. And this modest, courageous, upstanding woman became a true American hero.

Phan Thi Kim Phuc – The 9-year-old little girl who was playing at school when American troops dropped bombs in South Vietnam, June 8, 1972. Kim Phuc suffered burns over 75 percent of her body. The moment she went screaming into the streets, American photographer Nick Ut took her picture. After taking the picture, which was shown around the world and is believed to have helped end the war, the photographer scooped up the youngster, loaded her into his truck and rushed her to the hospital. His quick action helped save her life. Kim Phuc, now a mother and wife who lives in Canada, preaches and practices peace. On Veteran's Day in 1996, she read a statement at the Vietnam Veteran's Memorial expressing peace and the worldwide need for reconciliation and forgiveness. She even offered forgiveness for the man who dropped the bomb that burned her.

A. Philip Randolph (Excerpted and partially rewritten from pbs.org) -- Asa Philip Randolph was born April 15, 1889 in Crescent City, Fla., one of two sons of Rev. James William and Elizabeth Robinson Randolph, both descendants of slaves. The reverend required that his sons read books and religious magazines every day. With Chandler Owen, Randolph started THE MESSENGER, a radical Harlem magazine, in 1917. In August 1925, the Brotherhood of Sleeping Car Porters was officially launched. Randolph was chosen to lead the effort to unionize this company, one of the most powerful in America, because he was a great speaker.

Despite many setbacks over 12 years, the Brotherhood prevailed. President Franklin Roosevelt's New Deal legislation guaranteed workers the right to organize and required corporations to negotiate with unions. In 1937, the Brotherhood obtained a contract with the Pullman Company, the first contract ever between a company and a black union.

Randolph's next protest led to Roosevelt signing an executive order banning discrimination within the government and among the defense industries. July 26, 1948, Pres. Harry Truman issued an executive order barring discrimination in the military. By the early 1950s, Rev. Martin Luther King, Jr. came to the nation's attention. Randolph called for the March on Washington for Jobs and Freedom, August 28, 1963. Randolph, King, and others met with President Kennedy afterward. Within a year, the Civil Rights Act of 1964 was signed. Randolph died in 1979.

Harriet Tubman – Born into slavery around 1819 in Maryland, Harriet Tubman freed herself, and played a major role in freeing hundreds more slaves. After the Civil War, she joined her family in Auburn, NY, where she founded the Harriet Tubman Home. She was raised under harsh conditions, and subjected to whippings even as a small child. She is honored because she was not satisfied with getting freedom for herself, but put her life and her precious freedom at risk over and over again for years to free others through the secret network of the Underground Railroad.

As a teen, Harriet Tubman tried to stop a slave owner from catching a runaway. He threw an iron at her head. It hit her, and gave her a concussion, which caused her to have fainting spells, and pass out for hours. She knew that if she tried to escape slavery, she could fall asleep in the woods and be caught. But she wanted to achieve her dream of freedom so badly that she was willing to risk it. She thought about it all the time. Even after she married to a free man. He told her he would turn her in if she tried to run away, but she was so determined to be free that she was willing to run off and leave the man she loved to achieve it.